OWLY

THE WAY HOME

ANDY RUNTON

An Imprint of
SCHOLASTIC

Library of Congress Control Number: 2019936368

ISBN 978-1-338-30066-6 (hardcover)
ISBN 978-1-338-30065-9 (paperback)

10 9 8 7 6 5 4 3 2 1 20 21 22 23 24

Printed in Malaysia 108
First edition, February 2020
Edited by Megan Peace
Book design by Phil Falco
Publisher: David Saylor

FOR MY MOM

WHO BROUGHT THE JOY
OF THE LITTLE BIRDS
INTO MY LIFE

CONTENTS

FINDING HOME

?
HEY!
IT'S A BIG
BOWL OF
SEED!

IT LOOKS
SO GOOD!
I WONDER
WHO LEFT IT
FOR US.

WHAT'S
THAT?!
RUSTLE
RUSTLE

IT'S AN OWL!!!
SPILL!

OWLY JUST WANTED TO HELP...
seed

Seed

DINK
DINK

DINK DINK

DINK
DINK

?

HELP!
WE'RE TRAPPED!

LET'S GO!

OWLY JUST WANTED TO HELP...

Seed

IT'S NOT EASY FOR OWLY TO MAKE A FRIEND.

DRIP

DRIP
DRIP
DRIP

DRIP
DRIP
DRIP
DRIP
DRIP
DRIP
DRIP
DRIP
DRIP

HELP!

HELP ME!!!

SOMEBODY HELP! I CAN'T SWIM!!!
HELP!!!
HRMRMM...

SHIVER
SHIVER

OWLY RUSHES THE LITTLE WORM HOME TO GET HIM SAFE, WARM, AND DRY.
SHIVER
SHIVER

A WARM CUP OF TEA WILL HELP.

BUT SLEEP IS IMPORTANT, TOO.
ZZZ

OWLY

WHO-O-O
ARE YOU?

!

OWLY? M-M-MY NA-A-AME IS WORMY.

YUM!

THANK YOU FOR SAVING ME!

BUT, WHERE AM I?

WORMY

WORMY
I DON'T KNOW.

WELL, I REMEMBER...
DRIP
DRIP
DRIP
DRIP

CRRACK!
SPLASH!
!
!
!

NOW I'M LOST!
CAN YOU HELP ME FIND THE WAY HOME?
WORMIES
?

OWLY WANTS TO HELP WORMY, BUT HE DOESN'T KNOW HOW TO GET THERE.
?

BUT HE GETS AN IDEA!

WHAT ARE YOU LOOKING FOR, OWLY?

MAP

OWLY IS HAPPY THAT HE CAN HELP...

...AND WORMY IS, TOO!

THEY CAN FOLLOW THE MAP.
BUT IT'S A LONG WAY HOME.
MAP

OWLY KNOWS JUST WHAT TO PACK FOR THEIR JOURNEY.
SOAP
MAP

WORMY PACKS, TOO.

AND THEIR ADVENTURE BEGINS!

THEY SEE LOTS OF BEAUTIFUL THINGS.

BUT AFTER A WHILE, THEY NEED A LITTLE BREAK.

?
!
WHAT'S WRONG, OWLY?
!

AN APPLE IS A BETTER SNACK THAN POISONOUS BERRIES!

OWLY IS HAPPY
THAT HE CAN HELP...

...AND WORMY IS, TOO!

THE WOODS ARE SO DARK!

OWLY AND WORMY
MIGHT BE LOST.

THEY STOP TO CHECK THE MAP.

MAP

OWLY! IT'S A MONSTER!

JUMP!

SHIVER

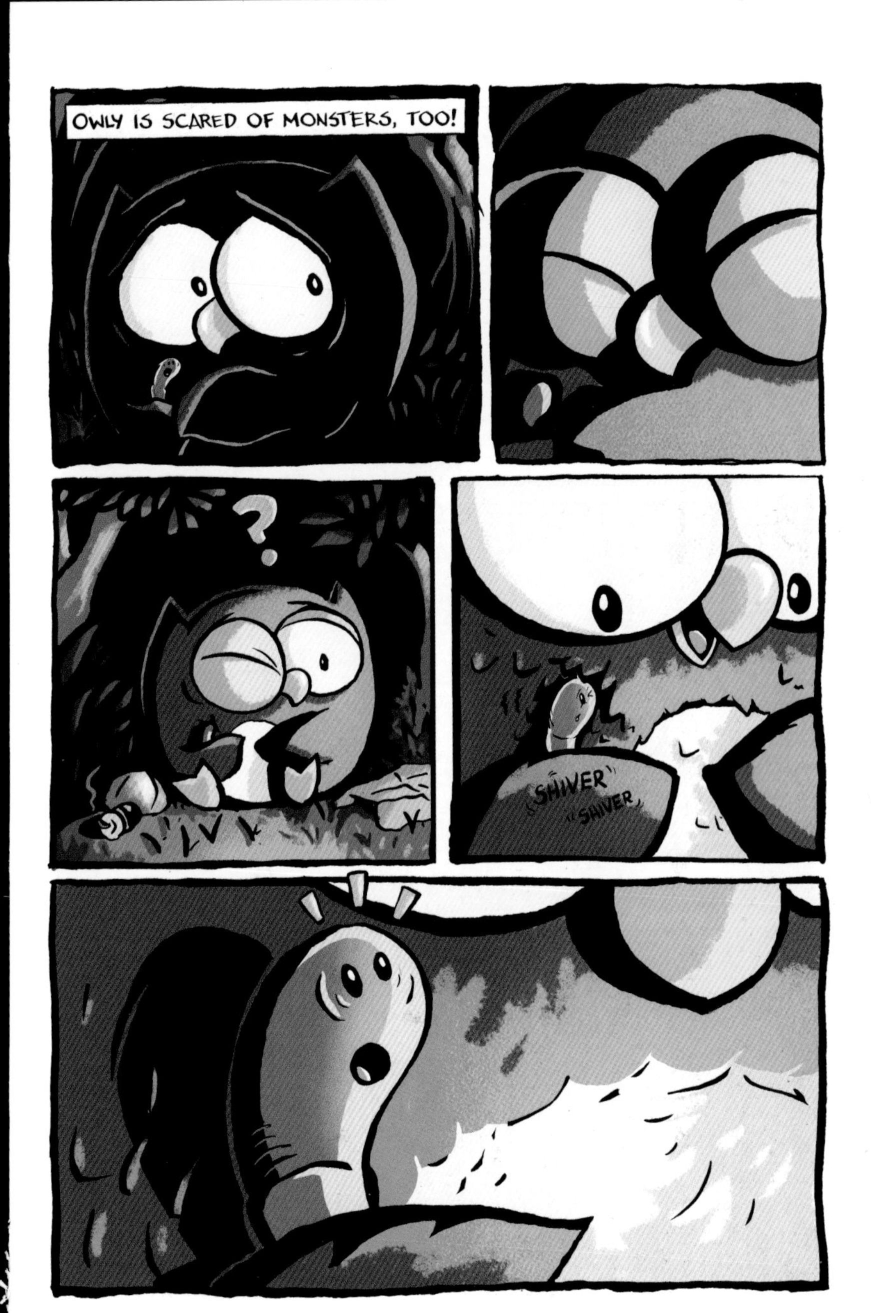
OWLY IS SCARED OF MONSTERS, TOO!
?
SHIVER
SHIVER
!!!

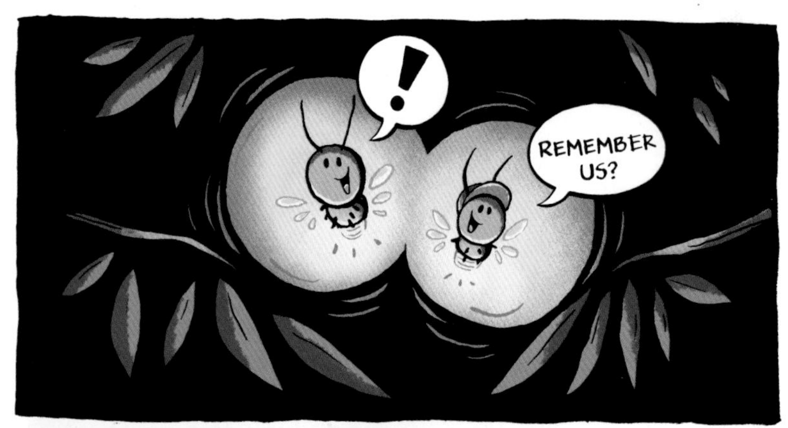
!
REMEMBER US?

THANK YOU!
SHAKE SHAKE

SORRY WE FLEW AWAY BEFORE.

CAN YOU HELP US FIND MY HOME?
?

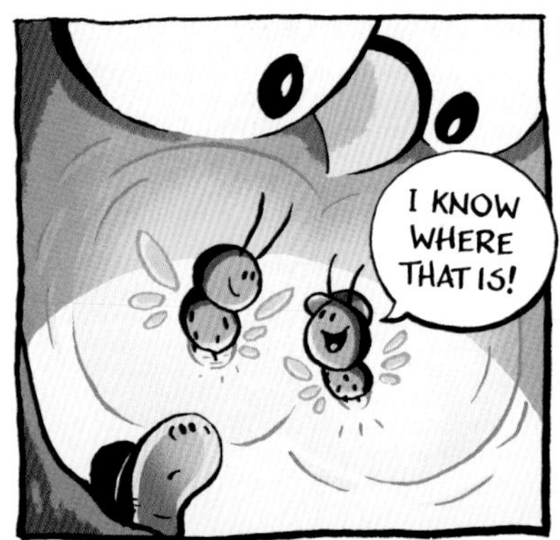
I KNOW WHERE THAT IS!

YOU DO?!
YEAH! FOLLOW US!

THE LIGHTNING BUGS HELP LEAD OWLY AND WORMY—
HOME!
THANK YOU!
SAFE TRAVELS!
GOOD LUCK!
!

MOM?
DAD?
??
THIS WAY!
!
!!!

OH NO! WORMY'S HOME IS GONE!
WO RMIES

SNIFF

MOM?
DAD?
??

WHERE ARE YOU?

TUMBLE!
TUMBLE!

CATCH!

SLIDE!

ROLL!

SPLOOF!

OWLY IS HAPPY THAT
HE COULD HELP...

...AND WORMY IS, TOO!

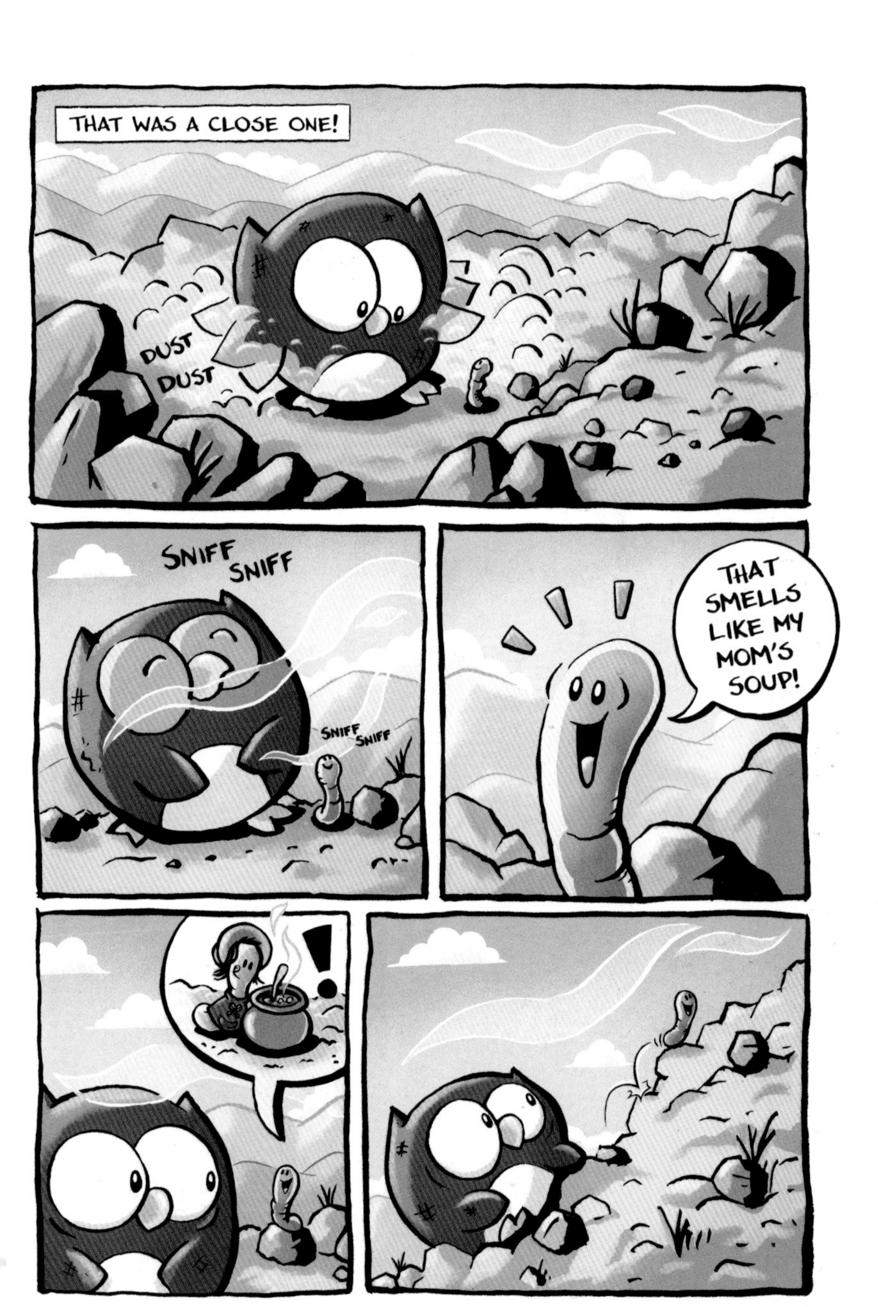
THAT WAS A CLOSE ONE!
DUST
DUST
SNIFF
SNIFF
SNIFF
SNIFF
THAT SMELLS LIKE MY MOM'S SOUP!

KNOCK
KNOCK
KNOCK
?
?

MOM! DAD!

WORMY!!! WE WERE SO WORRIED!

WHAT HAPPENED TO OUR HOUSE?!
?
IT WASHED AWAY IN THE RAIN!

OWLY!
!

SLAM!
WORMY!
OWLS ARE
DANGEROUS!

NO
OWLS!
!

SNIFF

BUT... OWLY IS MY FRIEND!

!

THANK YOU FOR HELPING WORMY!

SHAKE SHAKE

WILL YOU JOIN US FOR DINNER?
?

SOON IT'S TIME FOR OWLY TO GO HOME.

WORMY IS SAD...

...AND OWLY IS, TOO.

OWLY BEGINS HIS LONG JOURNEY HOME...

SCRUNCH

SCRUNCH
SCRUNCH
SCRUNCH

SCRUNCH
SCRUNCH

...BUT NOT WITHOUT WORMY!

OWLY, CAN I STAY WITH YOU?
?

?
FRIENDS SHOULD STICK TOGETHER.

LOOK! ANOTHER BOWL OF SEED!

THE
END

FLYING HOME

IT'S VERY SUNNY TODAY!

OWLY KNOWS HOW TO HELP!

THANKS, OWLY!
!

OWLY AND WORMY LOVE
WORKING IN THEIR GARDEN!

GOOD JOB GROWIN', LITTLE CARROTS!

HMMMZIP

?
!
OWLY!

HMMMZIP
I COULDN'T SEE ANYTHING!

WAS IT A BEE?

OWLY AND WORMY GET BACK TO WORK.

HMMMmm

MMMZIP
!!!

HMMMMMM

MMMZZZIP!

OWLY WANTS A CLOSER LOOK!

WHAT DO YOU SEE?

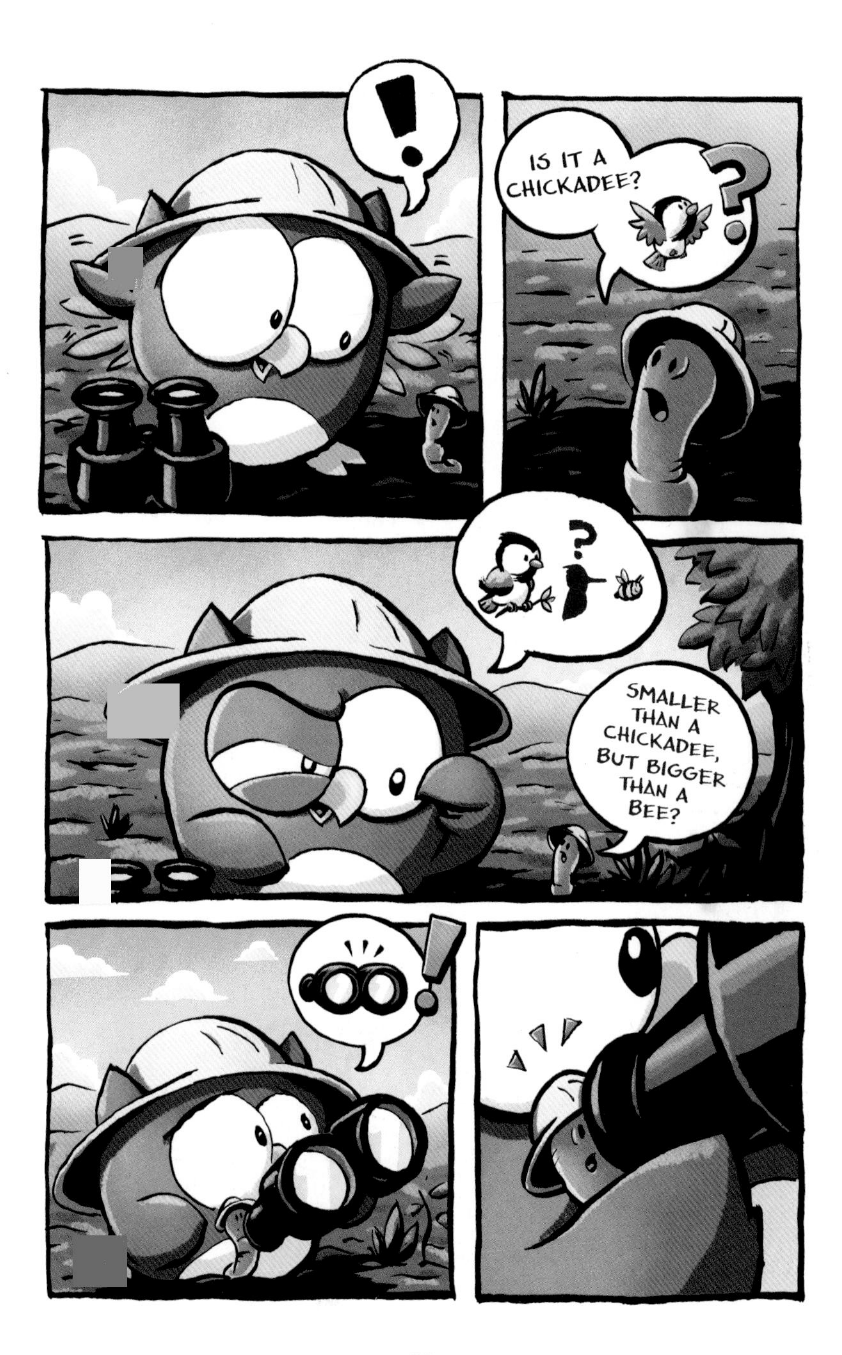
!
IS IT A CHICKADEE?
?
?
SMALLER THAN A CHICKADEE, BUT BIGGER THAN A BEE?
!

MAYBE HE'S HUNGRY?

OWLY AND WORMY WANT TO HELP.

LITTLE SEEDS
FOR LITTLE BIRDIES

HMMMMMMMM

MMMMMMMM

HI!
I'M WORMY!
HM
MY NAME IS TINY!
MMMMM

!

HMMMMM

I CAN'T EAT SEEDS.

?
HMMZIP

I WONDER WHAT HE CAN EAT...

OWLY AND WORMY GO HOME...

...TO FIND OUT WHAT TINY CAN EAT.

SMALL BIRDS

!!!

HUMMINGBIRDS
A MALE RUBY-THROATED HUMMINGBIRD IN FLIGHT.
HUMMINGBIRDS ARE THE SMALLEST OF ALL BIRDS. THESE TINY JEWELS OF THE SKY GET THEIR NAME FROM THE HUMMING SOUND MADE BY THEIR WINGS.
HUMMINGBIRDS DO NOT EAT SEEDS AND BERRIES LIKE OTHER SMALL BIRDS. INSTEAD, THEY FEED ON NECTAR FROM FLOWERS.

HE LIKES NECTAR!

LET'S BUY FLOWERS FROM MRS. RACCOON!

CLINKA

CLINKA
CLINKA
CLINKA

NURSERY
HI, OWLY!
HI, WORMY!
HI, MRS. RACCOON!
!

THERE ARE MANY FLOWERS...
$$
$$

LOCAL FLOWERS
$$

NECTAR FLOWERS

...BUT OWLY AND WORMY WANT TO FIND THE PERFECT ONE.

!

LANTANA
BLOOMS ALL SUMMER!
FULL SUN
$1.00

WAIT! WHAT ABOUT THIS ONE?

?

SALVIA
HUMMINGBIRD FAVORITE!
FULL / PARTIAL SUN

ARE THESE FOR A LITTLE HUMMINGBIRD?
?

THEY ARE!

!
GOOD LUCK! I HOPE HE LIKES THEM!

HMMMMMMmm

HMM
FOR ME?
MMM

SQUEAK!
SQUEAK!

HMMZIP

WHERE DID HE GO?
?

HMMMMMMMM
OWLY! TINY BROUGHT A FRIEND!

SQUEAK! SQUEAK!
HI! MY NAME IS ANGEL!
SHAKE SHAKE

SQUEAK! SQUEAK!
SQUEAK! SQUEAK!

SEE YOU TOMORROW! ENJOY YOUR FLOWERS!
NIGHTY NIGHT!

ZZZ
ZZZ

OWLY

HMMMM

? ? ?

OWLY! WORMY! HELP!
TINY IS TRAPPED!
TRAPPED?!

OWLY AND WORMY HURRY TO HELP!

THIS WAY!

HE'S OVER THERE!

GOOD
PLAN!

!
OWLY!
WORMY!

?
I'M READY!

!

NOW WHAT DO I DO?

GULP

I MADE IT!

?
RUSTLE
RUSTLE

?

SLIP

RUSTLE,
RUSTLE

RUSTLE
RUSTLE
JUMP!

IT WAS JUST A LITTLE BUNNY.

CLICK!

!

WHERE'S THE ROPE?

FLAP
FLAP
FLAP

!

CRASH!

TRIP!

THUD!

?!

!
I'M OKAY!

CREAK

LET'S GO!

OWLY AND HIS FRIENDS HURRY AWAY...

...TO THE SAFETY OF OWLY AND WORMY'S GARDEN.

IT'S PICTURE TIME!

CLICK!

Owly's
Owly
friends

Tiny, Wormy, and Angel
June 3

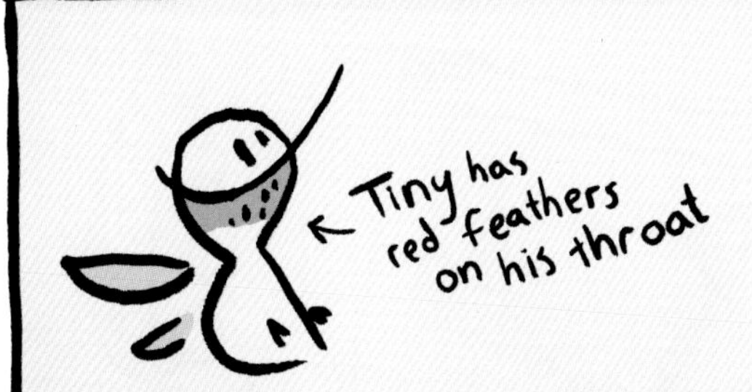

Owly, Angel, and Tiny

June 3

Tiny in his special butterfly bush
July 10
Angel enjoying Salvia – her favorite flower
SALVIA
HUMMINGBIRD FAVORITE!

Angel gets a sprinkle while
Owly gives the plants a drink

August 23

LANTANA
BLOOMS ALL SUMMER!
FULL SUN
$1.00
Tiny gives his wings a rest while snacking on the Lantana
Angel and Wormy play hide-and-seek in the flowers
September 23

Owly and Wormy in
the hummingbird garden.
It's getting a little chilly.
Fall is here!
Owly and Wormy's friends
always make them happy
October 5

OCTOBER

TAP
TAP

HI, ANGEL! HI, TINY!

WHOOSH

SHIVER
SHIVER

IT'S GETTING COLDER!

I'M ALL BUNDLED UP!
SQUEAK! SQUEAK!

WHOOSH

SHIVER SHIVER
TINY AND ANGEL ARE COLD.
OWLY AND WORMY WANT TO HELP.
!

NICE WORK, OWLY!

TIE TIE TIE

YOU'LL BE WARM NOW!

MMRPH
MMMRPH

!

THUMP
THUMP

HMMRPH
MMMRPH

THE SCARVES ARE TOO HEAVY.

THANK YOU, THOUGH.
FLUFF FLUFF
FLUFF FLUFF

IT'S GETTING COLDER...

...TOO COLD FOR THE FLOWERS.

I HAVE AN IDEA!

LET'S BRING THE FLOWERS INSIDE!

THANK YOU SO MUCH!

SQUEAK!
SQUEAK!

?
WHAT'S WRONG, OWLY?

LET'S GET MORE FLOWERS!

OWLY AND WORMY GO TO THE NURSERY...

NURSERY

LOCAL FLOWERS

...BUT ALL THE FLOWERS ARE GONE!
NECTAR FLOWERS
OH NO!

?
WE WON'T HAVE MORE NECTAR FLOWERS UNTIL SPRING.
APRIL
NOVEMBER
I'M SORRY.

HMMMMMM

DID YOU GET NEW FLOWERS?
?

WHAT CAN WE DO NOW?
IF WE GO SOMEPLACE WARM, THEN WE'LL FIND MORE FLOWERS.
?
FLOWER SEEDS
IT WILL TAKE TOO LONG FOR THOSE TO GROW.
FLOWER SEEDS

WE KNOW A PLACE DOWN SOUTH THAT'S ALWAYS WARM.

OWLY AND WORMY DON'T WANT THEIR FRIENDS TO LEAVE...

...BUT THEY KNOW THE FLOWERS WON'T SURVIVE THE COLD.

SNIFF

?
?

HAVE A SAFE TRIP!
SQUEAK! SQUEAK!

SNIFF

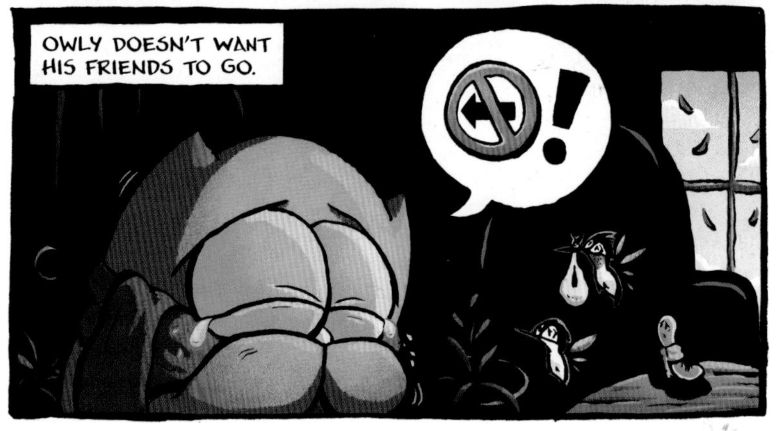
OWLY DOESN'T WANT HIS FRIENDS TO GO.
!

THEY CAN'T STAY INSIDE ALL WINTER, OWLY.

OWLY WILL MISS HIS FRIENDS.

BYE, OWLY!
BYE, WORMY!
SQUEAK!
SQUEAK!
SQUEAK!
OWLY
& Wormy
WE'LL MISS YOU!
WE'LL MISS YOU, TOO!

HUMMINGBIRDS

OWLY!
!

LOOK!
!

HUMMINGBIRDS
AS WINTER APPROACHES, HUMMINGBIRDS MIGRATE SOUTH, FOLLOWING THE BLOOMING FLOWERS.
THEY SPEND THE COLD WINTER IN SUNNY SOUTH AMERICA. MANY HUMMINGBIRDS EVEN FLY NONSTOP ACROSS THE GULF OF MEXICO TO REACH THEIR WARM WINTER HOME.
RUBY

NECTAR
FEMALE RUBY-THROAT ON HER NEST
EVEN THOUGH HUMMINGBIRDS MUST LEAVE IN WINTERTIME, AS SOON AS THE FLOWERS BEGIN TO BLOOM IN THE SPRING, THEY WILL RETURN. HUMMINGBIRDS HAVE AN EXCELLENT MEMORY AND ALWAYS RETURN TO THE SAME SPRINGTIME HOME.
MALE RUBY-THROAT
THEY'LL COME BACK!!!

!

OWLY AND WORMY HAVE A LOT TO DO BEFORE TINY AND ANGEL RETURN!
NOVEMBER
SEEDS

DECEMBER

JANUARY

FEBRUARY

MARCH

APRIL

WELCOME!

I SEE THEM!

SQUEAK!
SQUEAK!

THE
END

MORE OWLY ADVENTURES TO COME!

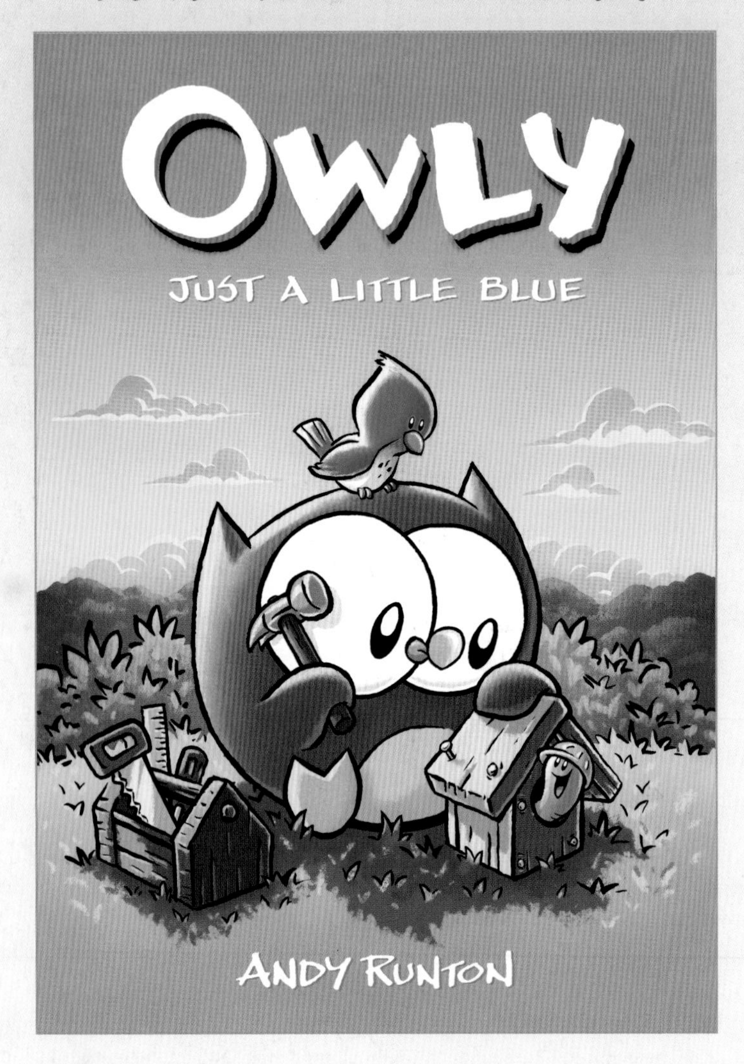

SPECIAL THANKS
TO ALL THE OWLY FANS
AND TO MY FAMILY AND FRIENDS
FOR THEIR INCREDIBLE SUPPORT!

ESPECIALLY TO RAINA FOR BELIEVING IN ME,
TO ANA & JILL FOR THEIR GUIDANCE,
TO BARRY FOR CHAMPIONING OWLY,
TO DAVID FOR NEVER GIVING UP,
AND TO MEGAN, PHIL, AND EVERYONE AT
SCHOLASTIC GRAPHIX FOR ALL OF THEIR
HARD WORK, GUIDANCE, AND FOR
WELCOMING OWLY INTO THE FAMILY.

COLORING ASSISTANCE PROVIDED BY
WES DZIOBA & PATTY RUNTON.
I COULDN'T HAVE DONE IT
WITHOUT THEIR HELP.
THANK YOU!

ANDY RUNTON

is the award-winning creator of Owly, which has earned him multiple awards, including the Eisner Award for Best Publication for a Younger Audience. The Owly books have been praised for their "charm, wisdom, and warmth" by *Booklist*, and WIRED.com said they are "one of the best comics for kids around. Period." Andy lives in the greater Atlanta area, where he works full time as a writer and illustrator. Visit him online at andyrunton.com.